THE SNOW BEAR

HOLLY WEBB

Stripes

THE
SNOW
BEAR

For more information about Holly Webb, visit:
www.holly-webb.com

STRIPES PUBLISHING
An imprint of Little Tiger Press
1 The Coda Centre, 189 Munster Road,
London SW6 6AW

This paperback edition first published
in Great Britain in 2012.

Text copyright © Holly Webb, 2012
Illustrations copyright © Artful Doodlers, 2012
Cover illustration copyright © Simon Mendez, 2012

ISBN: 978-1-84715-329-6

A CIP catalogue record for this book is available
from the British Library.

Printed and bound in the UK.

2 4 6 8 10 9 7 5 3 1

For Tom, Robin and William,
and for Phoebe, who loves polar bears.

~ HOLLY WEBB

CHAPTER ONE

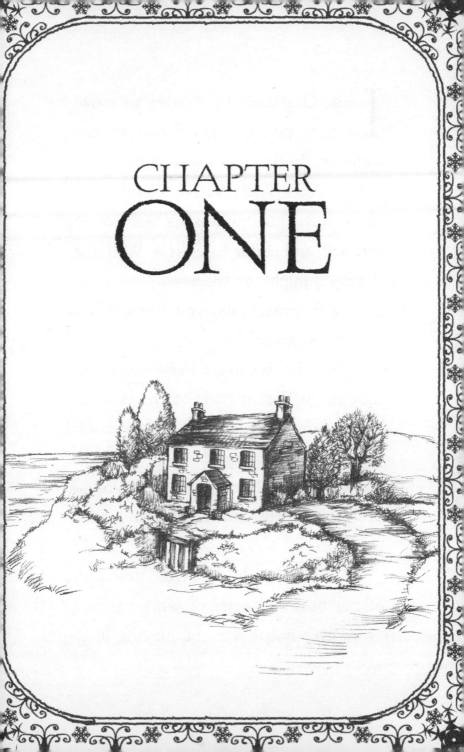

"Look, Grandad, it's starting to snow!" Sara peered out of the window, watching the first flakes spiral lazily down.

Grandad looked up from the pile of old black-and-white photos he was sorting through, and nodded. "So it is. Well, they did say it might, on the news."

Sara frowned. "Do you think it'll be snowing at home?"

"Could be. It's likely to be worse here, though. We're further north. And the winds from the sea make it a lot colder too." He got up and came to sit on the wide windowsill next to Sara. "Why are you looking worried? You love it when it snows!"

Sara nodded. It was true that some of her best memories of winter trips to Grandad's house were of playing in the snow. But then Mum and Dad had been there too. She couldn't have a snowball fight on her own.

"I hope it isn't snowing back home," she murmured, leaning against Grandad's shoulder. "What if the baby comes and Mum and Dad can't get to the hospital?"

"The baby's not due till after Christmas," he said comfortingly. "And anyway, they'd call an ambulance. Ambulance crews manage, you know. They're trained in that sort of thing."

"I suppose." Sara gave herself a little shake. There was no point worrying. She'd just remind Dad to put a spade in the car boot when he called later, that was all.

"It's settling!" she told Grandad, as she watched the flakes falling faster and faster. They were staying on the windowsill outside now, not just melting away as soon as they touched it. She wriggled closer to the glass, and peered up as the snowflakes whirled past. The light was fading, and the sky was a strange greyish-yellow colour, as though there was a lot more snow up there.

"Mmm. Looks like it," Grandad agreed. "I reckon I've done enough work for this afternoon. Shall we go and find something to cook for tea?" He kissed the top of her head, laughing. "It's all right. There *are* windows in the kitchen too. You'll still be able to see the snow. If it really settles, you'll be able to go out in it tomorrow. Too late now, though, it's getting dark already."

Sara slid down from the windowsill with a tiny sigh. She loved Grandad and his strange old house. It was a stone cottage, built more than two hundred years ago, and it had a huge fireplace and deep windows that were perfect for sitting in. All the floors sloped and wobbled, and it was full of strange little hidey-holes. But if she was at home, she'd get to go out in the snow with all her friends who lived close by. They'd build snowmen in the park and have snowfights, and then go back to each other's houses to warm up. But she didn't really fancy building a snowman all on her own, and it wouldn't be quite the same just with Grandad.

Sara and her mum and dad always came to Grandad's house at the beginning of the Christmas holidays. It was a tradition. They'd stay for a few days and then they'd all go back home for Christmas, Grandad too. But this year, Mum and Dad had decided it was better if Sara went to stay with Grandad on her own. Dad had driven her up, stayed for a quick lunch, and headed home again.

Mum wasn't in a state to be travelling far at all – she was due to have Sara's baby brother a couple of weeks after Christmas, and she didn't want to be squashed in a car for hours. Plus it wasn't very sensible for her to be in an old stone cottage on a cliff-top by the sea, down a long bumpy track, miles and miles from a village, let alone a hospital. Sara loved the feeling she got at Grandad's of being far away from anywhere. His house was like a safe little nest up on the cliff, like the seabirds' nests he'd shown her when they stayed in the summer. But she had to admit it wasn't the right place for Mum just now.

"Does it snow like this in the far north of Canada?" Sara asked Grandad, as she followed him out of his study, and down the murky half-light of the passage to the kitchen. Grandad had put the lights on, but it was still gloomy. "In the Arctic, where you and Great-Grandad were? Does it look like the same sort of snow?"

Grandad turned round from the fridge. "Snow's snow, mostly, Sara. We saw some real blizzards there, though. There was one that lasted for three days once, and we were caught by it while we were visiting one of the Inuit families. My dad and I had supplies back at our own house that we'd brought with us – tins of stew, that sort of thing – but these people were living on their traditional foods." Grandad paused, looking at Sara hopefully, waiting for her to ask. Sara didn't mind. She loved his stories.

"What did you have to eat?"

"Dried seal meat," Grandad told her triumphantly, pulling a bag of spaghetti out of the cupboard. He waved a jar of tomato pasta sauce at her. "Nothing like this. No pasta one day, stir-fry the next. With maybe a nice roast chicken on a Sunday. The Inuit mostly eat seal meat through the winter, and usually they have it raw. Perhaps some fish. Caribou meat in the summer. Whale meat and blubber too, of course."

Sara shuddered. Blubber was fat, and she hated the idea of having to eat it. She cut all the fat off her meat, and Grandad teased her about it. He said she'd be useless in a cold climate. "You *really* ate blubber?"

"We had to," Grandad nodded. "That blizzard lasted days. There wasn't anything else, and we were hungry. Besides, it would have been rude to say no. They were sharing their food with us. How could we say we didn't want it, when it was so precious?"

It seemed colder in the kitchen suddenly, and Sara shivered. The snow was building up round the corners of the window over the sink. She didn't want to think about being shut up with a blizzard screaming outside, even in this cosy house.

"Were you in an igloo?" she asked.

"Yes, a big one, made to last for the whole winter. It still wasn't any taller than your great-grandad, though. Almost all of it was the sleeping platform. And there were six of us in there."

"For three days..." Sara muttered. It couldn't have been bigger than her bedroom at home. "You must have been really grumpy with each other, being shut up all together."

Grandad smiled. "It helped me with learning the language, though. They told so many stories over those few days."

"Stories like the ones you're writing down?" Sara asked. Grandad was writing a book on Inuit folk tales. He'd been fascinated by them ever since he'd lived in Canada, when he was only a few years older than Sara. His father, Sara's great-grandfather, had gone there to study the Inuit people and taken his son with him. The house was full of the amazing things Great-Grandad had brought back, and Grandad too, when he'd returned to the Canadian Arctic years later.

Grandad nodded. "It was those three days of stories that set me off. When the blizzard finally died down and we came out of the igloo, it was as if they were all swirling around in my head. Some of them I didn't understand – there are lots of Inuit languages, and even your great-grandad didn't know all the different ones. I don't know them all now. I just got snatches of those stories here and there. Little snippets. Men who turned into polar bears. Strange gods and goddesses.

Amazing things…"

Sara smiled at him. "Tell me the polar bear story. The one about you and your friend, while you're cooking the tea. Please?"

"That one again?" Grandad laughed. "You're just like your dad. It was always his favourite as well."

Sara nodded. She loved imagining Grandad telling the story to Dad, too. It was a family story – it belonged to her, and Dad, and Grandad. It had been Great-Grandad's, too. It was special. "I wish I could go there, and see it all…" she murmured. "The igloos, and the seals, and the polar bears."

Grandad shook his head. "I shouldn't think you'd see an igloo now, Sara. Most Inuit people live in houses these days. Even back when Great-Grandad and

I were there, they were rare. That's why we went. We wanted to record it all, before it changed forever."

"Forever?" Sara asked sadly.

"I think so," Grandad agreed, with a sigh. "Things do change. But sometimes for the better."

CHAPTER TWO

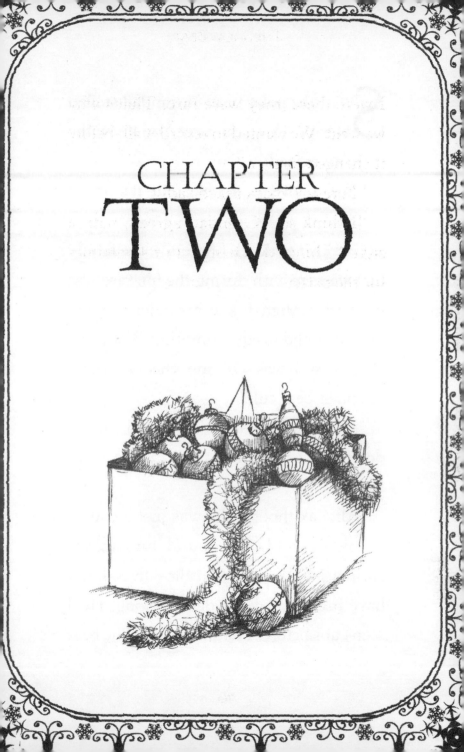

"So … the polar bear." Grandad smiled at Sara. "Are you sure? You know the story's a bit sad."

"Yes! I love it. I love that it's about you."

Grandad nodded. "Actually, the family that we were with during the blizzard was my friend Alignak and his older brother, his father and his grandmother. The same Alignak who was with me when we found the polar bear cub."

"How old was he?" Sara asked, sitting down at the kitchen table. "The bear, I mean."

"Alignak thought he was just a couple of months old. We found him in the springtime – he said that the cub couldn't have been out of his den for long. He'd seen cubs before. I hadn't a clue. The bear was just sitting in the snow, looking miserable."

"What were you doing, when you found him?"

Grandad laughed. "Well, Alignak was out to catch fish. I was along for the trip. He thought I was really funny. Useless at everything useful."

"And you found a polar bear." Sara giggled. "What did Alignak's mum say when he came home with a bear instead of fish?"

Grandad shook his head. "His mum had died, years before. It was a hard place to live, Sara. Alignak's grandmother looked after him, and his dad and his brother."

Sara nodded. "I remember now. Was she surprised, his grandmother?"

"Alignak had brought creatures home before – an Arctic hare, once. But never a bear. She told us to take it back. And Alignak told her he couldn't, because he'd used up all the dried fish she'd given him, coaxing the bear cub to follow us home. She was furious with him about that. But the bear stayed. Alignak and

I had to fish to feed him, and his father and brother gave us seal meat and blubber sometimes as well. I think he was probably too young for most of the things he ate. His mother would still have been giving him her milk. But he was hungry, so he made do."

"What did you call him?" Sara asked. She knew already, but she liked Grandad to tell her – it was part of the story.

"Peter. I named him, and Alignak liked the sound of it."

It was an old-fashioned sort of name, but Sara liked it too.

"What happened?" she asked quietly. This was the sad bit.

Grandad sighed. "We kept him all through the spring and the summer, and he got bigger. Alignak's father wasn't happy about the amount he was eating. He was taking food away from the family, you see. And they were worried that Peter might hurt us, I think, looking back. Never on purpose – he was friendlier than a dog. But even though he was only the size of a small dog when we found him, he was getting bigger and bigger, and he was strong. He'd jump up to hug us, and we'd go flying. He didn't really understand that his teeth and his claws were too sharp for playing." Grandad chuckled. "Actually, they weren't too sharp – it was just that we weren't bears. He should have been wrestling with his brother or sister. Polar bears usually have twins, and they grow up playing together."

Sara nodded. "So you had to make him go away."

"We tried to teach him how to catch seals, first. We didn't want him to be all on his own without being able to hunt. We showed him good places to find birds' eggs." Grandad leaned closer, showing her a tiny red mark at the side of his cheek. "See this scar? That's from an Arctic tern. They were dive-bombing us – you couldn't blame them, really. We were stealing their eggs. Peter loved them."

He sighed again. "It still makes me sad. We waited till the winter was coming – once the sea was frozen over, it would be easier for Peter to catch seals from the ice. He was nearly a year old then, we guessed, when we left him there. Just about old enough to manage by himself. Probably."

"But he'd have died if you hadn't taken him home with you when you found him,"

Sara said firmly. "You did the right thing."

Grandad nodded. "I know. And it wasn't fair to ask Alignak's family to look after a bear."

"Did you ever see him again?"

Grandad stirred the pasta thoughtfully. "We thought we did. There were quite a few young bears around that winter. But we could never be sure. I worried that he'd have gone too close to another polar bear, without realizing. They're loners, polar bears, once they're grown-up. Not friendly to each other. And after that winter, our year was up. We came home here again, your great-grandad and me." He glanced at Sara. "Come and watch this pasta for a moment. I've got something I think you'd like to see. I found it earlier on, mixed in with some other old things."

He went out to the study again, and came back a few minutes later with an old black-and-white photo. "Look."

Sara took it carefully. "Grandad! Is that you?"

"Mm-hm. And Alignak, and Peter. Sixty years ago, that must be now."

The boys and the bear stared out of the picture at Sara, smiling. Even the bear was smiling, she was sure.

Sara sat by Grandad's fireplace after tea, toasting in the warmth of the flames and gazing at the photograph, where Grandad had propped it up on the mantelpiece. The two boys looked so happy.

But seeing them just made her feel lonely.

Grandad was doing his best, but she really missed Mum and Dad. It felt so strange being at Grandad's house without them.

Grandad was out in the shed, finding the special big pot they were going to put the Christmas tree in. It was Sara's job to decorate it. But she needed Dad to help her get the tinsel right up to the top. And Mum always pointed out the branches that still needed baubles on. It just wasn't the same. Sara sniffed.

Iknik, Grandad's beautiful ginger cat, stalked into the room. He came over and sat down in front of the fire, close to Sara, but she was pretty sure it was the heat he wanted, not her. He wasn't really a friendly cat, although for some reason he would always sit on Sara's mum. Grandad said it was because Iknik was contrary, and he could tell that Sara's mum didn't like cats very much. Sara thought he was probably right. Still, *she* loved cats, and she kept trying with Iknik.

"Hey, Iknik…" she murmured. "Puss, puss, puss."

Iknik turned his head and glared at her with eyes that glinted reddish-gold in the firelight. They made him look fierce and Sara dropped her hand. She'd been about to stroke him, but maybe it wasn't a good idea.

"Found it!" Grandad called. He looked triumphant as he heaved in the huge pot. "You're in early, Iknik. He's usually out hunting this time of the evening, but maybe he doesn't like the snow? He's probably forgotten it since last year. Unless it's because I've lit the fire." He came over to rub Iknik behind the ears. "I originally called him Iknik because it means fire, you see, and he had such fiery marmalade fur, and those strange yellowish eyes. But it's an even better name than I meant it to be. Sometimes I worry he's going to singe his whiskers, but he seems to know just how close he can get."

Iknik purred and rubbed the side of his head against Grandad's trousers. Sara sighed. He wouldn't ever do that for her.

She stared gloomily into the fire. She wanted to be cheerful – she really didn't want to upset Grandad and make him think she wasn't having a good time. Especially as Grandad might worry and think he ought to call Dad. Which would make him and Mum worry about her, too.

But it was so hard to be happy, when she just wasn't.

Grandad put his arm round her shoulders. "Do you think it's time for bed? You might even wake up to find everything covered in snow…"

CHAPTER
THREE

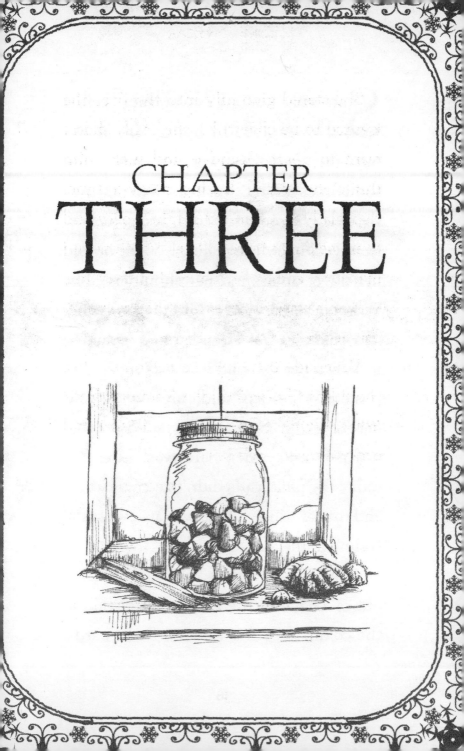

Sara woke up the next morning feeling cold. Grandad's house was lovely, but the radiators were ancient, and sometimes didn't work as well as they should. The room felt cold, and somehow *looked* cold, too, she realized, as she hauled her duvet up around her shoulders. The bedroom she slept in at Grandad's was her dad's old one, but Grandad had repainted it. When her dad had it, it was covered in posters, Grandad said, and you could hardly see the blue paint. He'd decorated it a pale pink when Sara was little. But today the pink walls didn't seem as warm and rosy as usual. There was an icy, crystal feeling in the air.

"The snow!" Sara squeaked, jumping out of bed, and then squeaking again at the coldness of the wooden floorboards.

"Ow, ow…" She hopped across the floor on her toes, dragging the duvet with her, and climbed up on to the windowsill. It was a large one, almost like a window seat, and she liked to curl up in it and read. She flung the curtains open, and took a deep, delighted breath. "Oh, look at it…"

Grandad's garden was very big, but usually Sara knew where everything was – the clumps of rosebushes, the wooden bench, the greenhouse. Now it was all just lumps and bumps. Even the greenhouse seemed to have been flattened out by the deep, sparkling snow.

She glanced round as the hall floorboards creaked. Grandad beamed at her from the bedroom door. "I might have known you'd be awake already. Amazing, isn't it?"

"It's so thick," Sara agreed. "I don't think I've ever seen snow like this."

"It must have snowed heavily all through the night," Grandad said, coming to stand at the window with her. "And the wind's been blowing the snow around too. It's all banked up against the garden wall, look, and the greenhouse."

Sara nodded. That explained why everything looked so strange. She hadn't thought about the wind, she'd just expected that snow fell straight down. But of course it didn't. It flurried about. "The wall looks like a ski-ramp," she said, giggling. "Can I go out in it, Grandad? I've got my big coat and my boots."

Grandad nodded. "Sure you don't want breakfast first? It might warm you up."

Sara shook her head. There was

something about the perfect glittering whiteness outside – she wanted to go and run about in it, and see her footprints. "I'll come back for breakfast in a little while. Is that OK? I just want to see what it's like."

Grandad nodded. "I think I'll make scrambled eggs. You'll need something hot. I feel cold enough just looking at all that snow."

"But it can't be as cold as it was in the Arctic," Sara reminded him.

"Mmm. I'm sixty years older than I was then, Sara. The cold seems to seep into my bones now. Still, maybe later on, when I've had some breakfast, I'll come out in it with you."

Sara hurried to get dressed, putting on her warmest jumper and trousers, and a pair of thick socks to go under her boots.

If she hadn't promised her mum that she really would clean her teeth every morning, she would have skipped that, but she felt too guilty.

Teeth brushed, she rushed down the stairs and opened the back door. The wind had dropped, and the air was very still. It made walking out into the garden seem dreamlike, it was so quiet. The snow had hushed everything. Even the sea, which Sara could always hear beating against the rocks when she stayed with Grandad. It was just a soft whisper in the background.

The garden looked like an illustration from a fairy tale. Sara had seen snow before, of course, but this was so deep, and so clean and new, that everything shimmered and sparkled in the thin, clear sunlight.

"I hope it doesn't melt," Sara said to herself, glancing up at the sky. But it didn't feel like it would. The sunshine hardly had any warmth in it, and she was cold, even wrapped up in her coat and long scarf. She stepped out on to the grass. At least, she thought it was the grass. She had to step carefully – she could have been standing on anything. Sara held out her hands to steady herself. She was glad that Grandad didn't have a pond – she might walk out into the middle of it in this.

"This is definitely the bit of grass between the roses and the wall," Sara muttered to herself, frowning and trying to remember the layout of the garden. She knew exactly what it looked like, almost as well as she knew her garden at home! But she'd never tried to walk round it blindfolded, and that was what it felt like.

The snow crunched and squeaked under her boots as she tracked across the lawn, admiring her footprints. It was about twenty centimetres deep, she thought. Not quite high enough to go over the top of her boots. But not far off.

Sara turned and looked back at her trail. The prints were really crisp, as though she'd shaped them with a knife. The snow was calling for her to build something in it. But not just a snowman. Somehow that wasn't right for the magical feel of the morning. Sara moulded a snowball thoughtfully, pressing it together between her gloved hands, and enjoying the feel of the snow under her fingers.

Then she smiled. Of course. Grandad's story last night. She was going to make a snow bear.

Once she had the idea, it came easily. The snow was a little powdery, but it held together well enough, and the shape she had in mind wasn't very complicated. Sara loved polar bears and she had lots of toy ones at home, of all sizes, and a little notebook with a polar bear photo on the cover. The bear was sitting up, almost like a boy slouching against a wall, with his hind paws stuck out in front of him. So it was easy enough to heap up a mound of snow to be his back, stretching it out into two fat back paws. The head was harder – when she tried to build the snow out into a pointed bear face, it just fell off. In the end she rolled a sort of triangular snowball, and balanced it on the top, with little snowballs for ears. Then she shaped some of the body into front paws, hanging down at the sides.

Sara stood back, admiring her bear. He was almost finished, but there was something missing. She pursed her lips thoughtfully, and then sighed. The eyes. She needed some little stones, or something like that – but everything was buried under the snow. She glanced around, and managed to find a couple of dark, withered rose leaves, still just about visible under the snow covering the bushes. She pushed them into place on either side of the long white muzzle, but they didn't look quite right.

Someone laughed behind her, and she turned to see Grandad standing in the doorway.

"He's fantastic, Sara!"

She grinned at him. "He is nice," she agreed. "But he isn't finished, Grandad. His face looks wrong. It's mostly the eyes. I can't find anything to make them out of."

Grandad nodded, and then rubbed his hands together. "I know. Give me just a minute." He hurried indoors, and came back, smiling, holding out a hand to her.

Sara tramped to the door, feeling the cold now that she'd stopped building. "Oh, they're perfect," she said delightedly, picking the bits of green sea glass from Grandad's hand. "I should have thought of that. Can I really borrow them? Won't they get lost in the snow?"

Grandad had a jar of sea glass on the kitchen windowsill, all shades of green, and even a couple of tiny blue pieces.

He picked it up when he went walking on the beach, and now, when the sun shone through it on the windowsill, it looked like a tiny jarful of the sea inside the house.

"Of course you can. You'll just have to go hunting on the beach for some more if they disappear when your bear melts. I'm sure we'll spot them in the grass, though."

Sara ran back to the bear, taking out the leaves and pressing the green glass into the snow. She smiled at the difference they made to the long white face. He was suddenly real, a snow bear sitting in the garden.

She couldn't help glancing back at him, as she hurried in to eat breakfast. She had the strangest feeling that he was waiting for her to return.

CHAPTER FOUR

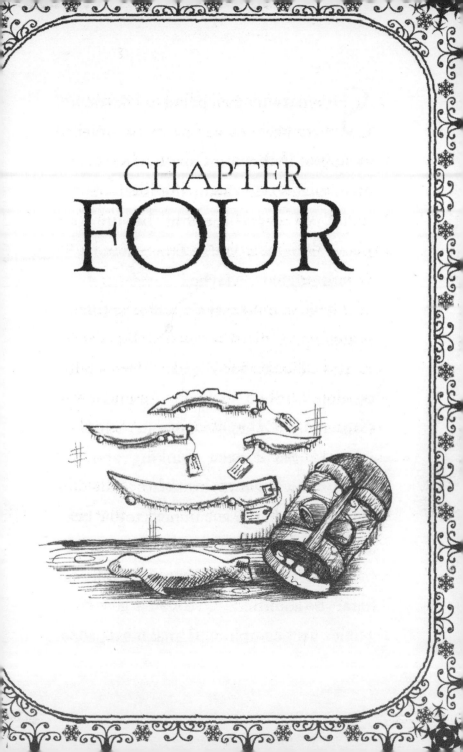

"So what are you going to do now?" Grandad asked, as they finished breakfast, both wiping toast crusts round their plates to catch the last of the scrambled egg. "I might be up to a snowball fight, if you're brave enough…"

Sara giggled. "Maybe."

"Or you could make a whole family of bears."

Sara shook her head. "No. One's enough." She looked hopefully at Grandad. "I'd really like to build an igloo…" She'd been thinking about it while she was eating breakfast – that she needed an igloo to live in next to the bear. It was all part of the story.

Grandad blinked. "I've never built one, Sara," he admitted. "I've watched it done, but it's very complicated, making a proper igloo. You have to stamp the snow down and then leave it to freeze before you cut the blocks out and build with them."

"Oh." Sara nodded sadly.

"But actually…" Grandad got up to look out of the kitchen window. "That snow that's been blown against the wall might be hard enough. Because the wind squashed it all against the bricks, you see."

"Really?" Sara asked hopefully, coming to stand on tiptoe beside him, peering out to look.

"Mmm. It wouldn't be a very long-lasting one," Grandad warned. "More of a quick shelter, the kind that Inuit hunters would build if they were away overnight."

"Any sort of igloo – I don't mind," Sara told him.

Grandad nodded, and put their plates in the sink. "I might even have something that would help," he murmured, and Sara followed him into his study. Grandad stood by the desk, looking at the collection of strange objects mounted on the wall behind it. Sara loved to look at them and try to work out what the faded old labels said – her great-grandad had very spidery writing.

"There it is!" Grandad said triumphantly, taking down a long, toothed knife, not metal, but made of something strange, hard and yellowish.

"What is it?" Sara asked.

"It's a snow knife," Grandad explained. "See if you can guess what it's made out of."

Sara stroked the smooth surface of the knife. It reminded her of teeth, and she frowned worriedly. "It isn't made out of elephant tusks, is it, Grandad? We were learning about ivory at school, and how people kill elephants, just for their tusks."

"Not quite. It isn't from an elephant, but it is a sort of ivory. Do you remember me telling you about walruses? They're a bit like seals, with big tusks."

"And that's what this is made from?" Sara said. She didn't like the idea of a knife made out of teeth.

"A long time ago. Your great-grandad brought this home, and it would have been very old even then. Walruses are protected now, but back then, hunters and their families used their bones and tusks after they'd eaten the walrus meat. They didn't waste anything. And this knife was for cutting out the blocks of snow to make an igloo."

Sara nodded. It looked a bit like the sort of plastic knife she used to have to cut her playdough with. She could see it would work on snow. "I wonder how many igloos it's made?" she said thoughtfully.

"Maybe hundreds. Let's make one more with it, shall we?" Grandad suggested, going out into the hall and slipping it into the pocket of his thick, padded coat. "I should think your great-grandad would be delighted. And whoever it was who made the knife."

They went out into the garden, and Sara patted the head of her snow bear, still sitting solemnly in the middle of the snowy lawn.

Grandad examined the bank of snow by the wall and nodded. "Good and solid, like I thought. Now we have to try and cut it into blocks with the knife."

Sara watched Grandad with the walrus-ivory knife – she still wasn't quite sure about it. She stamped around the snow they were going to build on, flattening it down, while Grandad started to cut out fat blocks of solid snow. It looked quite tricky to do, and Sara was glad they weren't trying to build a big igloo.

When they had the first few blocks, they laid them in a semicircle behind the snow bear, so that he would be sitting in front of the igloo.

"And now we just keep stacking them up…" Sara said, looking doubtfully at their ring of blocks.

"Yes, and they'll press in on each other as we curve them – that's the plan, anyway," Grandad agreed. He was looking excited about the project now, Sara realized.

Sara nodded. She had a feeling the igloo was going to be a lot of hard work. But it would be so amazing if they could really make one big enough to sit in.

After the first ring of blocks, they edged

them in a tiny bit, so that the igloo would
be dome-shaped, and then the next row a
little more. By the third row, the wall was
up to Sara's waist, and it was starting to
feel like a real little house.

"Wouldn't it be really dark inside if we were making one with just a tiny tunnel to get in?" Sara asked Grandad, panting a little as she helped him heave a block up to the height of her shoulders.

"Mmm," Grandad agreed. "They'd have an oil lamp, usually – burning oil made from seal fat. That made the igloo work better too, oddly enough. The heat from the lamp melted the snow on the inside just a little, and then it froze again harder, and that thin layer of ice stuck all the blocks together." He grinned at Sara. "We could try shining a torch on the inside of ours, but I'm not sure it would work. The Inuit would have used a seal's tummy to make a window. Stomachs are see-through, when you stretch them out! But I haven't got one of those, sorry."

"Uuughhh!" Sara gave him a disgusted look.

"We might be able to get some ice off the top of the water butt, if we feel like being clever. Some igloo-builders used ice for windows," Grandad explained.

Sara nodded excitedly. "I know we don't really need one, but it would make it even better." She swallowed, trying not to sound upset. "We ought to take some pictures of it, and email them to Mum and Dad."

Grandad put his arm round her. "Good idea. Your dad would have loved this – we did try building an igloo together once, but the snow was a bit too squashy." He chuckled to himself. "It collapsed all over me, and your dad couldn't stop laughing. We just had a snowball fight after that."

He sighed. "You're really missing them, aren't you?"

"Sorry," Sara whispered. "It just feels funny here without them."

Grandad nodded. "I know. Sara, love, this snow…" He stopped, looking at her worriedly, and Sara stared back at him.

"What?"

"I'm not sure I'm going to be able to take you home tomorrow."

Sara gasped. She hadn't even thought about that. But of course the roads would all be blocked by snow – the track up to Grandad's house was so narrow, and even the proper road wasn't very wide.

"What about Christmas?" she whispered. "It's only two more days…"

"Well, maybe it'll thaw," Grandad said, hugging her tighter. "Hopefully. But I can't promise that it will, Sara, even though I wish I could."

Sara nodded, rubbing her hand over her eyes. It was horrible, crying when it was so cold. The hot tears burned her eyes, and then felt like they were freezing on to her cheeks. "Can I go in?" she gulped, not looking up at him. The igloo wasn't done yet, but she couldn't finish it now.

"Of course you can! I'll come and make you some hot chocolate." Grandad sounded so upset, and that only made Sara feel worse. She bolted into the house, took off her coat and hat, scarf and boots as fast as she could with frozen fingers, and ran upstairs. She was really cold, but she didn't want a drink. She looked around her room uncertainly, and then dived back into bed, hiding herself under the duvet.

She heard Grandad opening her bedroom door a few minutes later, but he didn't say anything, and then the floorboards creaked as he slowly went away again.

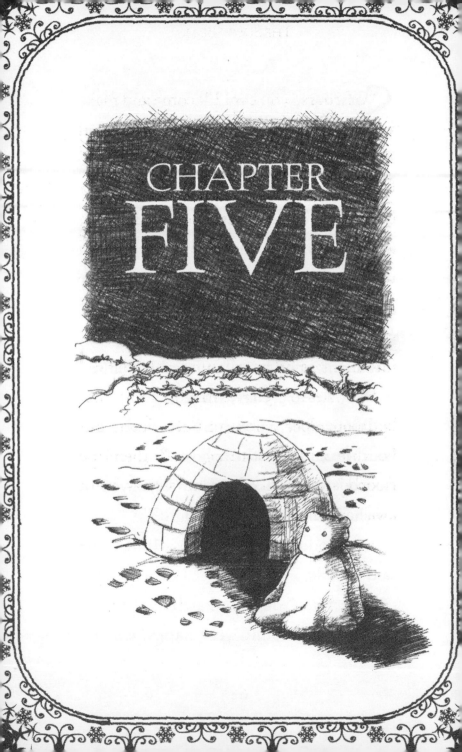

CHAPTER
FIVE

"Sara?"

Sara yawned, and half hiccupped. And then realized that she'd been crying, and remembered why. She wriggled out of the duvet, and sat up blearily. "Hi, Grandad."

"Are you all right?" Grandad asked her anxiously.

Sara sniffed, and nodded sadly. She was, just about. She was still miserable, but she didn't want to cry any more.

"You've been asleep a long while, and your mum's on the phone." Grandad passed it to her. "Come down when you've finished talking to her, all right?"

Sara nodded again. "Hi, Mum," she said huskily.

"Oh, Sara. You sound awful."

"You don't sound very happy, either."

Sara laughed sadly.

Mum sighed. "Silly, aren't we? Your grandad said he explained that you're going to have to stay for now. He doesn't think it's going to thaw out any time soon."

Sara shook her head, and then remembered her mum couldn't see her, and whispered, "No."

"But try not to get upset. We'll wait and have Christmas with you, Sara. We'll put it off until you're back. I'll make your dad eat pasta and salad on Christmas Day."

Sara giggled. "That's mean!"

"Maybe sausages, then. Oh, sweetheart, I really miss you! Promise me you'll try and enjoy the snow with your grandad. He says he'll get you home as soon as it's safe. But I wouldn't want him to do anything silly."

"Is it snowy there, too?"

"A bit, but nothing like what you've got. I'd better go, sweetheart, I've got to see the midwife. I just wanted to ring and say hello."

"Thanks," Sara sniffed. "I hope it goes OK. Love you, Mum…"

"Love you, too."

Sara pressed the end call button, and sniffed hard a couple more times, trying not to start crying again. It helped that Mum hated it when Sara sniffed – she always told her to blow her nose. Sara could just about manage to laugh at that.

She still felt sad as she walked downstairs, and put the phone back in its cradle in Grandad's study.

He popped out of the kitchen, eyeing her anxiously. "Are you feeling any better?"

"Mmm. Mum says she's going to save

Christmas until I'm there, if she has to."

"What about something to eat? You missed lunch. Sandwich? Toast?"

Sara shook her head. She wasn't hungry at all. She didn't really know what to do with herself – she'd promised Mum she wouldn't be miserable, but it wasn't easy. In the end, she got a book and curled up in the armchair in the study, watching Grandad work and trying to read. She didn't get very far. Most of the time she just stared at the strange things all over the walls. They were covered in photographs of her grandad and great-grandad on their travels, and the things they'd brought back, like the ivory knife. There was even a canoe hanging from the ceiling.

Sara only picked at her tea – even though Grandad had made her favourite, eggy bread and bacon. Then she went up to bed early, but she couldn't sleep – she'd slept too much earlier in the day, and now she felt jumpy and tired at the same time. In the end she got out of bed, and sat on the wide windowsill, staring into the garden.

The igloo was glowing in the winter moonlight, and Sara smiled sadly. It was finished – Grandad must have finished it for her while she was asleep. The entrance was an arch, and at the back of the igloo she could just about see that he had made her a window – he must have found some ice.

Her snow bear looked strangely real, sitting by the igloo with his fat paws dangling sleepily in front of him. Sara wondered if he would move, if she sat still and watched for long enough. Then she shook her head crossly. Now she was just being silly. She'd go downstairs and get a drink, she decided. Some milk. Maybe that would help her sleep. She pattered down the stairs and into the kitchen, glad she'd put her dressing gown on. It was freezing.

Grandad was standing by the kettle, making himself a hot drink. "You can't sleep either?"

Sara shook her head. "I was sitting by my window, looking at the snow bear and the igloo," she murmured.

"What about if I told you another story?" Grandad suggested.

Sara nodded, and then glanced up at him hopefully. "Would you tell it to me in the igloo? I haven't been in it yet – you finished it, and it looks so beautiful."

"You don't mind that I did? I thought it might cheer you up."

"It has." Sara leaned her head against his arm. "And it looks perfect for telling stories in."

Grandad sighed. "It'll be too cold, Sara! What would your mum say?" He gave her a sudden, worried look, as though he thought he shouldn't have mentioned her mum. "But I suppose, if we put on our warmest things – and took sleeping bags, and a groundsheet…"

"Yes!" Sara hugged him. "And can we have biscuits? For a midnight feast in the snow?"

Grandad rolled his eyes. "Go on, then. I'll make some sandwiches as well."

Sara nudged him. "Prawn sandwiches?" Grandad always had prawn mayonnaise sandwiches – they were his favourite, and now Sara loved them, too.

"Mmm. Go and get me those sleeping bags out of the cupboard under the stairs…"

Sara lay snuggled in her sleeping bag, watching the stars tangled in the snowy branches of Grandad's apple trees. The igloo wasn't big enough for Grandad to lie down in, but Sara could, if she curled up a bit. And the wide arch of the entrance framed the sky, perfect for stargazing. Her mum could see those same stars at home, Sara thought, blinking sleepily. Mum loved to sit in their little glass conservatory and look up at the stars, even in winter, when the conservatory was freezing. Sara was suddenly sure that her mum was there at that very moment. She found it really hard to sleep, now that she was so big, and it wasn't all that late. Only about eleven.

Sara smiled. It was the nicest thought she'd had since Grandad had broken the news.

"What are you smiling about?" Grandad nudged her gently.

"That Mum's probably watching these stars, too, out of the conservatory roof. Right now." Sara gave a satisfied little sigh.

Grandad nodded. "You're probably right. They're amazing, aren't they? Always the same. On and on, forever and ever. Or it seems that way to us, at least. I was looking at these same stars with Alignak and Peter, sixty years ago…"

"Tell me the story," Sara murmured, wriggling closer in her sleeping bag, so that she could lean up against him. "Properly, this time. The way you always start it…"

Grandad wrapped his arms round her. "All right." He gave a little cough, clearing his throat, like a real storyteller. "Once upon a time, during the Arctic spring, when there was snow and ice all around, and the days were starting to get longer…"

Sara sighed happily, and closed her eyes to listen. That was just right – the proper beginning to the story. Grandad's voice rumbled, wrapping around her and warming her, the same way his arms did. And the story went on…

CHAPTER
SIX

S ara blinked sleepily, and gazed out of the arched entrance of the igloo, into the strange, purplish light. She hadn't meant to fall asleep, and it was colder than ever. She looked round for Grandad, thinking that he must have fallen asleep, too, but he wasn't there. Sara struggled up out of her sleeping bag, and pulled her boots back on, meaning to hurry into the house and find him.

But as she sat there, tugging at her boots, Sara realized that everything had changed. She hadn't slept in the igloo all night – Grandad would never have let her. So how could it be light? Or almost light, anyway. The snow around her igloo was glimmering in the light of an odd, pink-streaked sky, as though it was early morning.

The house was gone. They'd built the igloo facing towards the house, she knew they had. But it wasn't there any more – and neither was her snow bear. Her boots on at last, Sara crawled out of the igloo and stood up. She stared around, eyes wide.

She wasn't in Grandad's garden at all.

Snow stretched around her, for as far as she could see. There were no houses, not even any trees, just mounds and hummocks and mountains of snow, with here and there a patch of rock or scrubby grass showing through. Sara looked back at her igloo. It was definitely still there, and so was her sleeping bag, and the bag of sandwiches and chocolate biscuits. But her snow bear had gone, which just made everything seem even stranger.

She was dreaming. She had to be. But it was strange to be in a dream, and *know* that it was a dream. Tugging her coat more tightly round her shoulders, Sara stepped out into the snow, shivering a little. It was the coldest dream she had ever been in, too.

She looked around, wondering if there was anyone to talk to, to tell her where she was, and called, "Hello…" She didn't call very loudly. She felt shy, somehow, shouting into all that whiteness. And only the wind answered her.

Sara took a few steps round the side of the igloo. She had some odd idea that on the other side of the snow house she might find the way home, that there might be a sort of door back to Grandad's garden. But she forgot all about that when she came round the back of the igloo and found her snow bear.

He was standing now, on all four paws, but he still only came halfway up Sara's legs. He stared at her uncertainly, with round dark eyes – not green glass any more – and Sara stared back. His eyes had changed, but it was her bear. She knew it. She knew *him*.

He was *real* – soft and furry. She wanted desperately to stroke him, he looked so like her cuddly polar bears back home. But this was a real bear now, a wild bear. Sara shook her head, wondering how this could possibly have happened. Then she smiled to herself. She didn't understand it at all, but she'd heard so many of Grandad's stories, and wished and wished she could see the places he talked about. And now she was in the Arctic!

The cub was looking at her, as though he didn't know what she was, Sara thought. He might never have seen a human before. She looked round anxiously. The bear cub was only small – she wasn't really sure how old – but she guessed he was probably only a few months. So he shouldn't be on his own. Somewhere close by, there would be an enormous mother polar bear, looking for her baby.

Even though Sara thought polar bears were lovely, she knew how fierce they could be. She watched nature programmes about bears, and she had books about them, and Grandad had told her loads of stories. They lived mostly by hunting seals, but polar bears could hurt people, too, when they found hunters on their own, or if they thought humans were attacking their cubs. Her little igloo wouldn't be much protection against an angry polar bear.

Sara started to back away slowly, wondering where the mother bear was. She thought it was probably better not to run – polar bears were much faster than people, she was sure. But the polar bear cub gazed after her anxiously, and then took a couple of little steps towards her.

Sara stopped, biting her lip. Was he lost? She was sure that a cub wouldn't usually be away from his mother like this.

The cub ventured closer and gave a whine, a tiny noise that sounded more like a puppy than anything Sara had expected from a bear. She couldn't leave him, she realized. He was too little, and he was scared. She had to help him, somehow. Which was silly, because she thought he probably knew a lot more about surviving in the Arctic than she did.

"Do you need me to help you find your mother?" she said gently, coming a bit closer.

The bear looked up at her hopefully, and she sighed. "I don't know where she is. I don't even know where I am, actually. But that must be why I'm here, in this dream, if that's what it is. To take you home."

Sara walked slowly and carefully back to the igloo. The little bear looked hungry, she thought, and she had her sandwiches. She had a feeling he was too young to be eating mostly seal-meat, like an adult bear. He was still supposed to be feeding from his mother. But in the Arctic cold, he needed to be fed, even if that meant eating prawn sandwiches. Otherwise he wouldn't have the strength to go far.

"Bet you've never had anything like this," Sara muttered, undoing the foil Grandad had wrapped round the sandwiches. "I suppose it's lucky they're prawn. I shouldn't think you'd like cheese and ketchup – that's my other favourite."

Even though the bear surely hadn't

heard the crinkle of silver foil before, he seemed to know at once that it meant food. He padded over the snow towards Sara, and stopped just a step away, looking hopefully from Sara to the foil packet and back again.

Sara laughed, and then felt guilty as he skittered away. "Sorry! I didn't mean to scare you," she whispered. "Yes, they're for you, that's why I opened them. Come on, come and try. You'll like it. Prawns are yummy."

The bear sniffed hopefully, and looked around, as though he thought he probably shouldn't be doing this, and his mum might suddenly turn up and tell him off. But when Sara tore off a little piece of sandwich and held it out, he couldn't resist. He snatched it out of her fingers, and gulped it down greedily. Then he came closer, looking for more.

"I told you you'd like it," Sara murmured, feeling pleased. "You'd better not have too much, you're not used to this kind of food. Oh…"

The bear didn't agree. He barged close in to Sara, nudging eagerly at the packet, and rootling around in the foil.

"OK, OK. You're really hungry. I know. Here, look, have some more." Sara looked at him worriedly as he gobbled the sandwiches. "I wonder how long you've been on your own. You're still lovely and plump, you can't have been hungry for all that long…"

Gently, while he was still eating, she slipped off one glove and stroked the back of his neck. She was prepared to pull her hand back quickly in case he didn't like it, but he didn't seem to mind. He just glanced at her quickly, checking what she was doing, and then went back to the food.

"We'd better find your mother fast," Sara said, sitting down and rubbing the soft folds of fur round his neck. "I've just got Grandad's sandwiches now, and after that it's only chocolate biscuits left. I don't think

I can give you those, I should think they're really bad for you. I know chocolate's bad for dogs. I bet it's not good for bears, either." She shivered. She shouldn't have taken her glove off, but she'd so wanted to feel his fur. Her hand was aching with the cold now, and she felt shivery.

She put the glove back on, and carefully patted the bear, rubbing behind his ears and tickling him under the chin, like she tried to do with Iknik. The bear was a lot friendlier, especially now that she'd fed him. He licked all round his jaws – Sara got a glimpse of his teeth, which were quite big, even though he wasn't – and he sniffed her gloves, to see if she was bringing more food.

"I need to give you a name," Sara said thoughtfully. "I can't just call you bear."

She ran her hand over his domed white head, and the bear nuzzled at her wrist. "Oh! Of course." She smiled. "I'll call you Peter. Like Grandad's bear." She shook her head, suddenly confused. "Maybe you *are* Grandad's bear? Maybe I'm taking you back to your mother, so the boys don't have to leave you on the sea-ice at the end of the summer?" Sara frowned. "But that would be silly. How can I be inside Grandad's story? And it's not a dream, I'm sure it's not. You're real. I can feel you. You can't feel things the same way in dreams…"

She stood up, looking around anxiously. How was she going to find a white bear in all this snow? "Maybe you can find her," she suggested to Peter. "Polar bears hunt by smell, I'm sure I read that. Can you follow your mother's scent? Can you track her? Or maybe you're just too little."

Peter stood next to her, quite close, his soft head almost resting on the side of her coat, so that she could feel the warmth of him. He seemed to be waiting for her to tell him what to do, Sara thought. He was used to following his mother.

"I wish we had some idea where to go," Sara muttered. "What if I head in the wrong direction, and just take you further away from her?"

Peter put his nose down, and snuffled thoughtfully at the snow, looking up at Sara with dark, sparkling eyes.

"What is it?" She bent down to look, and took in a quick, excited breath. "Tracks! Aren't you clever?" The tracks were hard to see – she'd never have spotted them herself – but they were definitely there. And they were too big to be Peter's own paw prints – they were fat heavy pads pressed into the loose snow, setting off across the whiteness, like a trail to follow. "She must have lost you, somehow, and gone off looking for you. We just have to catch her up," Sara said firmly. She picked up the little bag of sandwiches and biscuits, and started to follow the prints of the big-footed bear, leading the cub out into the snow.

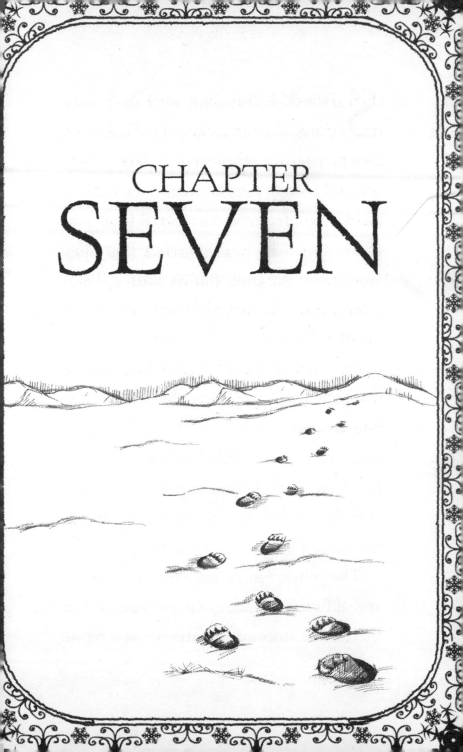

CHAPTER
SEVEN

Sara and the bear followed the tracks. It was a strange way to walk, eyes down, peering at the faint paw prints. Every so often, they seemed to fade away, as though fresh snow had fallen over them, and Sara was worried that they would lose the trail. But each time, Peter would sniff around, and come across the tracks again.

Sara huddled the hood of her coat up round her ears, wishing she'd put more sweaters on underneath. She'd thought it was cold at Grandad's, but it was nothing like this. She pressed closer to the bear cub, feeling the warmth of his fur under her gloved hand as they walked on.

The white landscape was very quiet, and at first Sara thought it was empty. But then Peter stopped in surprise as a white creature raced over the snow in front of them, stopped for a second to look, and dashed away as the bear cub made a strange, cross grunting sound.

Sara gazed after it, trying to see what it was as it skipped from patches of snow to the darker tundra that was showing through. It looked like a fat, old-fashioned powder puff, with a pair of long, dark-tipped ears. "An Arctic hare," Sara murmured, as it disappeared into the distance. The dark eyes and nose looked like pebbles against the snow, and the hare blurred as it ran – its camouflage was perfect. She remembered seeing a photo of a hare in one of the books she'd read about polar bears. But there hardly seemed to be enough green stuff around for it to eat. Just mossy patches here and there.

"It would help if you could eat this, too," she said to Peter, crouching down to look at the yellowish lichen. "I think I'd better save the second lot of sandwiches a bit longer, just in case."

The polar bear cub sniffed at the lichen, and looked up at her so disgustedly that she had to laugh. "I don't think I'd like it, either," she admitted. Then she shivered again. Was it really growing colder? She wasn't certain what time of year it was here – she was pretty sure the Arctic would be completely covered in snow in winter, which meant this had to be spring or summer. But it was so cold, and it was starting to snow again, she realized in dismay, watching the snowflakes start to float gently down. They were so pretty and delicate – but there were so many of them, and they were falling faster and faster. Sara took a sudden tight grip on Peter's fur. She could hardly see him now, a white bear in a white whirling snowstorm.

"It's a blizzard," she whispered, the cold stealing her voice away. "We can't stay out in this. We'll freeze…"

Peter tugged at her hand, and she gasped, frightened that he'd run off, and she would lose him. But he looked back up at her, his dark eyes glinting among the snowflakes. He wanted her to follow him.

Step by step, half blind, Sara followed the little bear to a strange cave, a dark hole in a snowdrift that appeared suddenly out of the storm. Peter dived inside and then turned round, seizing Sara's coat in his sharp little teeth, and dragging her after him. Sitting down inside the earthy burrow, away from the biting wind, Sara gasped, trying to catch her breath. The cold seemed to have frozen her lungs. Peter snuggled up next

to her and sniffed hopefully at the bag of
sandwiches. Sara fumbled at it, and tore
off a little piece of sandwich for herself,
feeding the rest to the bear cub. Then
Peter curled up half across her lap and
nudged her lovingly, before he fell asleep.

Sara stared out at the dark snowstorm,
wondering what they were going to do
now. Perhaps another of these sudden
blizzards had blown up before, and that
was how Peter had been separated from
his mother.

The cub sighed in his sleep, and Sara stroked his white fur – he was nearly as fluffy as that powder-puff of a hare. He was so young, and he trusted her. She had to get him back to his mother. But as Sara gazed out into the storm, she knew that all his mother's footprints would have been covered long ago…

Sara fell asleep too, eventually – the flickering fall of the snowflakes was hard to watch without her eyelids starting to close. When she woke up, it had stopped snowing, and the landscape stretched out into whiteness in front of her.

Peter woke, wriggling, and bounced over to the little tunnel's entrance hole, peering out at the snow eagerly. Maybe he was hoping to see his mother, Sara thought sadly, watching him stick his head out.

She blinked, suddenly realizing where they must be. This was a maternity den, where a mother polar bear had hidden herself over the winter, digging down through a snowdrift to the earth below, to make a safe nest for herself and her babies. It was probably where Peter had been born. He must have sniffed it out, catching his mother's scent in the storm. Maybe he'd been making for the den when Sara found him.

Sara followed him out into the snow, looking around hopefully for the paw prints. She knew they must have been covered up, but still… Peter sniffed at the fresh snow, looking up at her in confusion.

"I know," Sara murmured. "We'll just have to find your mother another way. It'll be all right."

The little bear ran off into the snow, kicking up the fresh powder with his claws, and squeaking. Sara giggled. Even though she was worried, she couldn't not laugh – he was so funny, dancing about in the snow. He didn't seem to feel the cold as much as she did. His fur was perfectly designed for the Arctic weather, Sara thought to herself. She couldn't even feel her fingers properly any more. She shook her head, as if it might help her feel less dopey with the cold.

Peter stopped sharply and gave a little growl, staring down at the ground. He'd found something. Sara hurried over to him, clapping her hands together to try to warm them up.

Tracks. But not bear tracks – these were long, thin grooves, with smaller paw prints here and there. A dog sled. Sara felt her heart jump with excitement – they weren't alone in the snow, as she'd thought. Perhaps whoever had driven past in the sled would have seen Peter's mother, and would be able to tell her where to take him.

They set off again, following the sled tracks this time. The sled must have passed by their den since the snow stopped falling, Sara realized. It couldn't be that far ahead of them, although it would be moving much faster than they were. There was still a chance they could catch up. Perhaps the sled might stop for the dogs to have a rest? If only she could keep walking. She was so tired, even though they must have slept for a long time in the den, and it seemed an effort just to lift her feet. Peter was tiring quickly, too. He'd slowed down, and he kept looking up at her hopefully and nudging at the food bag with his nose.

"No more sandwiches," Sara told him apologetically. "Maybe if we catch up with the sled, whoever's driving it will have something for you." Then she stopped, staring out across the snow, her heart racing.

That noise – a low, mournful howling. She'd heard it before, but only in films, never for real. It was a noise from the kind of films where she liked to hide behind her mum on the sofa, with her dad teasing them about being scared.

It was a wolf.

Peter gave her a frightened look and darted sideways.

If he was with his mother, Sara thought, he'd be fine. She'd scare the wolves away. Sara had only heard one howling, but it wouldn't be alone. Wolves travelled in packs. They wouldn't attack an adult bear, especially one with a cub to protect – she would be too fierce, too risky. But a girl and a bear cub – they were easy prey. Sara hadn't any way to fight back, not even with Grandad's ivory knife. Had the wolves caught their scent? The noise seemed to be coming from a distance. Perhaps if they were lucky...

The howling came again, and Sara realized with dismay that it was in front of them – on the same course as the tracks. To stay away from the wolves they'd have to turn aside, and lose their chance of catching up with the sled.

But they didn't have a choice.

CHAPTER EIGHT

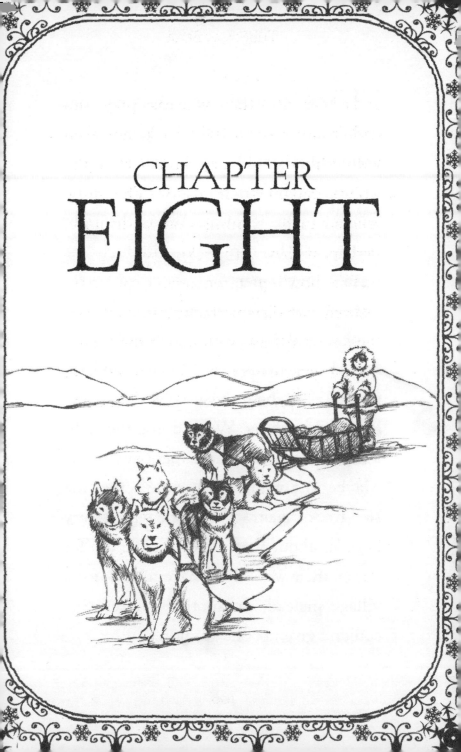

They hurried on, striking out sideways from the tracks, Sara hoping that would take them away from the wolves. The howling seemed a little fainter and further away. At least the fright had woken her up a bit, although she wasn't any warmer.

Peter was whimpering now, tired and hungry, and Sara stopped to stroke him, and whisper in his ears. "We have to keep going. What about those wolves? We can't let them catch us. We're doing the right thing, Peter. I can't hear them any more. Maybe in a while we'll come across the sled tracks again..." But she wasn't very hopeful about that. They'd gone too far out of their way. She'd have to look for a village instead, or another hunter. She couldn't give up. She wouldn't.

Eventually Peter simply stopped, shaking his head like a sulky child, refusing to go any further.

Sara looked at him anxiously. "What's the matter? Are you hurt? Come on, little bear. We can't just stop. We'll both freeze."

But Peter stayed where he was, his paws planted stubbornly in the snow, shaking his head, and making that odd chuffing little growl again.

Sara sighed. Maybe he'd follow her if she went on a bit. He was tired, that was all. She took a few steps away from him, hoping he'd stop being grouchy and catch her up. She turned back to see if he was going to follow, and smiled as she saw him start to run forward. It was working!

Her sigh of relief turned to surprise as Peter yipped worriedly, and caught her trouser leg in his teeth – but too late. She was already falling. A crevasse in the ice had opened up beneath her, and she hadn't even seen it. *Peter must have known,* she thought wearily. She seemed to be turning over and over as she tumbled into the darkness, and everything was horribly slow. *He sensed something was wrong. He wasn't being sulky. He was trying to stop me. I should have realized…*

Her head hurt. Sara tried to sit up, but that only made her feel sick and dizzy, and when she opened her eyes, everything went white.

She blinked.

Actually, everything *was* white. She'd forgotten for a moment, that was all. She was in some strange world of dream and snow, trying to return a lost polar bear cub to his mother. And now she had fallen into a crevasse, a great tear in the ice. How far down was she?

She peered up again, more carefully this time, trying not to jar her aching head. Peter was looking down at her, a white furry head leaning over the edge of the icy cliff, eyeing her worriedly.

He was a long way up. Perhaps an arm's length further than she could reach. She couldn't get back up there, not without a rope, and someone to pull. The ice looked sheer – there were no useful little footholds to climb up by. She wasn't sure she could climb even if there were – she felt all wobbly.

Peter whined worriedly, and Sara tried to stand up, to tell him it was all right. But she had a horrible feeling it wasn't. She was stuck.

She blinked again. There was another face now, another furry face, staring down at her over the lip of the crevasse. She squinted, half closing her eyes against the low sunlight, and realized that it was a boy, wearing a fur-trimmed hood. An Inuit boy, a few years older than her. Peter had edged away from him, but he was still there.

"Did you fall down?" the boy called.

Sara nodded, and wished she hadn't. "Yes," she whispered, wincing. It was a stupid question, anyway. What did he think had happened?

"All right. Don't worry. I just need to undo some of the harness, then I can use it to pull you out."

"Thank you…" Sara said quietly, wrapping her arms round her middle. It was even colder down in the crevasse, although at least she was sheltered from the wind. She could hear it whining and whistling as it blew over the top of the great crack in the ice.

What did the boy mean, harness? She thought of calling back to ask, but didn't. She didn't want to slow him down.

"Can you tie this round yourself?" A strip of dark stuff that looked like oiled leather was dangling above her, and the boy's face was staring down at her. She could see his mittened hand, too, guiding the harness so it fell towards her.

Of course. It was his sled they'd followed, and those strange whining noises weren't just the wind. There was a team of sled dogs up there, and he'd unfastened their harness so he could use it to pull her out. They must have wandered close to the sled tracks again after all. Sara tied the harness round her waist, and held on to it as tightly as she could. She wasn't sure how the boy was going to pull her out. He looked bigger than she was, but not that much bigger. Surely she would be too heavy for him to manage on his own?

"Hold on! We'll start pulling you up now," he called down to her, and Sara gasped as the harness tightened, and she started to bump slowly up the icy wall. He was using the dogs to help him drag her up – she could hear their claws scuffling on the ice, and their confused whining as they pulled this strange load.

The ice wasn't quite as smooth as it had looked from down below, and Sara was able to push herself up a little by digging her toes into the cracks here and there. But it was still a slow and difficult climb, and she was exhausted by the time the boy hauled her over the lip of the crevasse.

"Thank you!" she gasped, and then let out a breathless laugh as Peter hurled himself at her, nuzzling her anxiously. He kept sniffing and nudging at her, obviously trying to make sure she was all right.

"So he's yours? You've got a polar bear cub?" the boy asked her curiously as he untied the harness and fixed it back on to the sled with the six dogs jumping around him excitedly. "How did you find him?"

Sara shook her head very carefully.

Her headache wasn't as bad as it had been before, but it was still definitely there. She must have hit it as she fell. "He found me," she told the boy. "He's lost. I was trying to help him find his mother, but the snowstorm covered her tracks." She staggered, almost falling, and the boy grabbed her arms.

"You look frozen. Here, sit down on the sled. Wrap these round you." He half led, half pushed her to the dog-sled, grabbing a bundle of soft, greyish furs that Sara thought were probably seal skin. She felt sorry for the seals, but they were beautifully warm!

"That's better." The boy nodded approvingly. "You're lucky I saw your bear cub. There's a wolf pack close – I heard them howling."

"We heard them, too," Sara whispered, huddling herself into the furs.

"Look, eat some of this." The boy undid one of the packages tied to the sled. "You need to keep eating out here. You have to keep your strength up in the cold."

Sara looked at the strange, leathery stuff he was trying to feed her, and nibbled a little bit of it politely. It was horrible. It tasted fishy and oily and dry, all at the same time. She guessed it was some sort of preserved fish. She burrowed under the seal skins for the bag of food she'd brought from home, and dug out two chocolate biscuits. She handed one to the boy, and he looked at it as though he'd never seen anything like it before. "Maybe you've never had chocolate? You'll love it. Oh, my head hurts…"

The boy was looking at her worriedly, but he was eating the biscuit, and obviously liked it. Sara sneaked her piece of dried fish to Peter, who she'd pulled up next to her on the sled. He needed it more than she did, she told herself, feeling a little bit guilty. Peter didn't seem to mind the taste at all, and he snuggled up next to her under the seal skins, casting nervous glances at the dogs. They were a bit bigger than he was, and very loud. The boy had fastened their harnesses back on, but they weren't lined up in pairs, the way Sara had expected. Instead they were harnessed in a sort of fan shape in front of the sled. They kept turning round and staring at Sara and Peter with bright, inquisitive eyes.

Sara looked at the boy, licking chocolate from round his lips eagerly. He seemed familiar, somehow. But she couldn't work out why. Her sore head was making everything seem strange, and it was only as the boy climbed on to the sled in front of her and called to the dogs, sending them racing over the snow, that Sara wondered how she could understand what he was saying. She'd been talking to him all this time, and she was sure they weren't talking English.

CHAPTER NINE

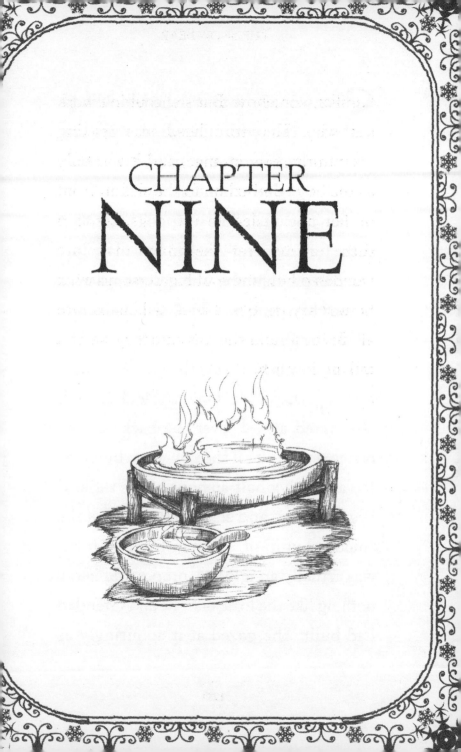

Sara was about to ask the boy who he was, but with the wind whistling around them, and the snow crunching under the sled runners, she knew he wouldn't hear her. She wrapped herself up in the furs more tightly, and leaned against Peter. Now that she was getting warmer again, her fingers throbbed painfully inside her fleece gloves.

Where was he taking them? Somewhere warm, perhaps. He'd said she looked cold. She stared ahead, over the backs of the racing dogs, but all she saw was whiteness. It was another half an hour before the sled began to slow, and she understood that the smooth hump of snow in front of them was actually an igloo. A proper, big igloo, nothing like the little one she and Grandad had built. She gazed at it admiringly as they pulled up by the side, and the sled dogs immediately started barking excitedly.

This igloo had a proper entrance tunnel, half buried in the snow. The igloo was taller than Sara was – she guessed it was about the same height as her grandad, maybe a little taller. It was built of huge blocks of snow, each about half a metre long, and fitted together perfectly. It shone in the pinkish light, and Sara smiled at the sight of it. She hadn't ever thought that an igloo could be so beautiful.

The boy sprang down from the sled, and started to unharness the dogs, and fasten them to posts dug into the snow. He saw that Sara was watching him questioningly. "They sleep outdoors."

"Won't they be cold?" Sara asked, looking at the dogs anxiously.

But the boy only laughed and pointed to the nearest dog, who was curled up in the snow, with his tail wrapped tightly round his nose and his paws. Sara had never seen a dog curl up so small – he looked almost like a cat. "They can sleep through a blizzard like that. And they have to stay out – they're our guard dogs, too. They let us know if there's a polar bear around."

Sara hugged Peter tightly. "They won't hurt him, will they?"

The boy shook his head. "No, I don't think so. He's too little. And perhaps he smells of you."

The boy finished tying up the dogs, and came towards her, holding out a hand to help her off the sled. "You'd better come in. You need feeding. My grandmother will make you some soup – that'll warm you up. My father still isn't back with a seal, and you look too cold to wait." He hauled her off the sled, and Peter leaped off after her. Then the boy ducked down, stooping into the entrance of the igloo, and waving at her to follow him.

Sara laid her hand on Peter's neck, calling him to follow, but he wasn't sure about going into the little tunnel. Perhaps the igloo smelled strangely of humans. He sniffed at it doubtfully and looked up at her. Then at last he gave himself a little shake, as though he'd decided it must be all right, if she was going in. Together they crept inside the snow house.

As Sara emerged into the main room of the igloo, blinking in the dim light, the boy seemed to be arguing with someone.

"You see! I'm sorry I didn't bring back any fish, but I'm not telling a story, I did find a girl," the boy said triumphantly, coming to pull her further in. "She'd fallen into a crevasse. I saw the bear cub first. I wanted to know why he was staring over the edge of the ice like that." Proudly, he

turned Sara to face an old lady, sitting on
a pile of skins spread over a ledge of snow
that ran across the far side of the igloo. She
was wrapped in skins too, with a sort of
furry poncho over a bright fringed and
embroidered tunic, and a pair of the same
soft furry boots that the boy was wearing.
She was sitting by a strange bowl-shaped
lamp full of oil, and sewing by the light it
gave her.

The old lady shook her head. "A girl
and a bear. Like one of the old tales,
Alignak, you're right, though I could have
done with those fish." She turned to Sara.
"Where have you come from, child? And
who sent you out dressed like that? You
look half frozen." Frowning, she tugged at
Sara's coat sleeve, as though she didn't
approve of it at all. "Come here, sit by the

qulliq. Maybe you came from the lights," she whispered. "One of the ancestors, come down from the sky..."

"It feels warm in here," Sara said, as she sat where the old lady showed her, holding out her hands over the stone oil lamp. Grandad had talked about lamps like this, hadn't he? That they melted the inside of the igloo? She looked up at the snow wall and saw that it was a sheet of smooth ice, like he'd said. But she hadn't expected the igloo to feel so cosy, when it was made of snow! There was even a block of greenish ice, halfway up the wall, for a window.

The old lady bustled around, finding some more dried meat and putting it into a small stone pot that she balanced on a frame over the lamp. "Go and get me some snow, Alignak," she told the boy.

"I'll make some broth to warm her up."
Then she eyed Peter thoughtfully. "I've no
fresh seal meat for you, little one, not till
my son and Alignak's brother come back
from hunting. You'll have to have the
dried caribou, like your girl." She cut off a
strip, and fed it to Peter, who was lying
across Sara's feet. She was actually starting
to be able to feel her toes again, and she
was thinking more clearly in the warmth.
Who did Alignak and his grandmother
think she was?

And who were they?

Then she remembered. That was where
she knew him from! The photograph!

Alignak was the boy her grandad had
known, she was sure. The boy who'd been
with him when he found the bear cub.
It was as though she was inside her

favourite story. Sara shook her head. She didn't understand, and she didn't think Alignak and his grandmother did, either. But perhaps it didn't really matter. The important thing was to find Peter's mother, and make sure he was safe. Sara sat watching the orange flames flickering on the oil lamp, and feeling Peter shift and wriggle on her feet as he gnawed at the dried meat.

The broth in the stone pot was starting to steam gently. It smelled like the tins of beef and vegetable soup her dad liked to have when it was cold. Sara bit her lip. She didn't want to think about home – it was too far away – but it was hard not to. Dad might be having soup for lunch too.

"Here." Alignak's grandmother passed her a wide ivory spoon, and beckoned her to sit by the cooking pot. "This should warm you up."

Sara sipped the broth, blowing at it, and wincing as it burned her lips. After the dried fish, she hadn't been sure she'd like the soup, but it was hot and delicious, and soon she could feel the warmth spreading through her. She offered the spoon to Alignak, but he shook his head.

"No, you eat it. My father and brother will be back soon, with a seal."

While Sara was eating, the old lady was searching through a pile of clothes, glancing over at Sara, and muttering to herself. She turned over soft furs, and more of the beautiful embroidered tunics that she was wearing. Sara had seen photos of Inuit people dressed in clothes like these back at Grandad's, but they'd all been in black and white. She hadn't expected the clothes to be so brightly coloured.

As soon as Sara had finished the soup, Alignak's grandmother held up a pair of mittens and a hood, and nodded. "These should fit. Take off those other ones – they're no use at all."

Sara obediently slipped her fleece gloves into her pockets, and put the fur mittens on.

"They're caribou skin," Alignak told her. "Much warmer than yours. Caribou makes the best snow clothes."

Sara nodded. The mittens felt warm and soft. The Inuit people used every part of the creatures they hunted, Grandad had told her, even the stomach and other insides. Nothing was wasted. She might not have wanted to wear fur at home, but here, in this strange snowy dream, she knew she needed the mittens. The old lady tied the hood round her chin and looked pleased.

"Thank you," Sara whispered, reaching down to stroke Peter, who was pulling at her leg with his teeth.

"He wants to go," Alignak said, and Sara nodded.

"But we don't know where we're going," she sighed. "The storm buried his mother's tracks. How am I supposed to find her?"

Alignak frowned. "She'll be further out on the sea ice, where the seals come up," he told her, glancing at his grandmother, who nodded. "Hunting. There's a lead, not too far from here, where we often see bears."

Sara shook her head apologetically. "What's a *lead*?"

The boy blinked, as though he couldn't believe she didn't know. "Open water – like a channel in the ice. Bears like to hunt there, you see. We hunt there too, sometimes. I can show you which way to go…" He looked as though he'd like to go too, but his grandmother was shaking her head.

She probably doesn't want him to get gobbled up by an angry mother polar bear, Sara thought to herself, shivering a little, even with the warm mittens and hood. *Or maybe she thinks I'm some sort of strange creature out of an old story.*

"You should wait for my son to come back," the old lady said firmly. "Alignak's father. He'll take you – that will be safer."

But Peter was pulling at her leg again, and making anxious little growling noises. He seemed determined that they go now. Sara smiled gratefully at Alignak and his grandmother. "I can't wait – it's starting to get dark, isn't it? I'll have no chance of finding Peter's mother then."

She didn't want to say it, but if she waited for the hunters to get back and take her to the lead, they would probably frighten the mother bear away. Or worse, she might know what hunters looked like, and decide to attack them. It was safer for everyone if she and Peter went by themselves.

"Thank you for the soup, and for feeding Peter," she told the old lady. "It was very kind of you."

"We always share what we have," Alignak said, sounding almost surprised. "Food belongs to everyone who needs it. Come on, I'll take you towards the break in the sea ice – just a little way," he added to his grandmother, who nodded reluctantly.

"I wish I could come with you all the way," Alignak said as they came out into the snow again, and he led her towards the ice hills behind the igloo. "But the bears – it's too dangerous, unless we're in a hunting party." He looked at her worriedly and caught her hand, as though he wanted to pull her back to the safety of the igloo. "I have to go back. Will you really be all right?"

Sara swallowed and nodded firmly. "Yes." She was fairly sure she couldn't be eaten in a story. Almost sure, anyway. She hugged Alignak, surprised at how small he felt under his layers of furs, and laughed at his shocked face. "Goodbye!" she called as she walked away, turning back every so often to wave. Peter galloped ahead of her, full of energy now that he'd eaten.

The last time she turned back, Alignak and the igloo seemed to have melted away, settling back into the snowy whiteness, as if they had never been there at all.

CHAPTER TEN

Had it only been a trick of the fading light? Sara almost ran back to see, but something stopped her. It was better to keep going, and Peter was darting ahead of her. She hurried after the little bear – she couldn't risk losing him.

To get to the lead, where Alignak thought Peter's mother might be, they had to walk through a maze of strange ice hills, where the ice had been squashed up over the years till it looked like waves on the sea. It was hard going, picking her way through the icy hummocks, and Sara's legs were aching. Peter's furry feet and sharp claws were built for scrambling over ice, and he kept bouncing along in front of her, turning back every so often to run round behind and herd her along, like a lost sheep.

"I know. You want to see your mother. Soon. I'm sure we'll find her soon," Sara muttered, stopping to rest for a minute. "I hope so, anyway," she added, glancing anxiously at the sky. It was getting dark, the low sun striking the ice formations and turning them a glowing pink. It was beautiful – but scary. What if they had to spend a night out here on the ice? They could try to find their way back to the igloo, but they'd already been walking for ages, and it would be fully dark before they got back. If the snow house was even still there.

She shivered suddenly as an eerie howl echoed around the snowy hills. The wolves were back. Peter slunk closer to her, pressing anxiously against her legs. She should have asked Alignak for a bow and arrows, Sara thought, biting her lip. She wasn't sure how far they were from the lead – Alignak had said it was an hour's walk. It felt like they'd been walking for longer. Perhaps they were close. It would be so unfair if the wolves drove them off-course again.

Maybe she could throw a stone – except there weren't any. A chunk of ice? She scrabbled around at her feet, trying to find something, anything, she could use as a weapon.

Then a low, threatening growl made her stop, her breath catching in her throat. Was that the wolves? Were they closer? She stood up slowly, trying to push Peter behind her. Perhaps the wolves would be so surprised to see a human they'd run off, especially if she shouted. She couldn't let them hurt the little bear.

But then Peter darted forward, making excited little squeaking noises, and Sara gulped. An enormous polar bear was running towards them, so fast that she was swinging from side to side.

Sara felt her eyes fill with joyful tears,

and she rubbed an icy mitten across her face to brush them away before they froze. They'd found her! The huge white bear was Peter's mother. It had to be, from the way he was leaping joyfully around her.

The big bear sniffed him carefully, all over, making sure he was all right. Then she nuzzled him lovingly, rubbing her huge head up and down his soft fur again and again. At last, she looked up, staring curiously at Sara. She took a step towards her, and Sara realized that the mother bear's paw prints in the snow made hers look tiny, even though she had her big boots on. Sara had got used to thinking of polar bears as Peter-sized. Small and cuddly. This bear was taller on all four paws than Sara was standing up. If the bear stood up on her hind legs to fight, she'd be giant.

THE SNOW BEAR

Sara swallowed. She wasn't sure if the bear knew what she'd been doing – that she'd been trying to help. What if Peter's mother thought she was dangerous, that Sara was someone who might hurt her baby? She stood still, looking down at her small feet, and trying not to seem scary.

But the bear didn't come any closer. She nudged Peter firmly, and turned around, heading back the way she'd come. Peter glanced back at Sara and hesitated, but followed his mother. They set off across the snow, leaving Sara all alone.

She'd done it. She'd brought Peter back to his mother.

Sara tried to smile, but she felt too tired and too sad. She'd only known the little bear for a day, but now he was gone, she felt lost. She sank down slowly, so that she was sitting in the snow. She knew she shouldn't – if she sat down, she'd get too cold. She had to keep moving. She had to find her own way home now.

She'd only sit for a little while. Tears ran slowly down her cheeks, and she felt them freeze. A few snowflakes drifted gently past her.

Then someone nudged her, a gentle push against her shoulder, and Sara looked up slowly.

They were back. Peter's mother was standing over her. So close that Sara could see her eyes, black and glinting and curious. She nudged Sara again, shoving her so that she'd stand up. Sara staggered to her feet obediently, and the bear seemed to be pleased. She crouched down in the snow, stretching her forepaws out in front of her, and pushed Sara up against her side.

Sara looked worriedly at Peter. Did his mother want her to climb on to her back? Peter darted towards her, and pushed the back of her knees. Sara did as she was told, clambering on to the huge back, just behind the bear's shoulder. She'd ridden a pony before, but the bear was so big, and so wide. It was like sitting on a sofa – a warm, white, slightly smelly sofa that moved. Sara gave a squeak as the bear set off, swaying gently as she walked. Peter ran along beside them, looking up at Sara happily, and occasionally dancing off in front of his mother to snap at the snowflakes and scuffle about, just like a little boy.

Sara stared around her. It was almost completely dark, and a light snow was falling. The sky was scattered with stars, and she smiled sadly, remembering the stars in Grandad's garden and at home. How was she going to get back?

She frowned a little, staring at the sky – a strange, greenish-white band had appeared, stretching across the stars, and as she watched, it grew. The light stretched into a curtain that seemed to be hanging in the sky, rippling and shimmering. Purple streaks danced across it, and Sara laughed in delight.

The polar bear stopped, gazing up at the lights and nuzzling her cub.

"The Northern Lights," Sara whispered. "Grandad told me about them. I wish I could go back and tell him I've seen them too…" She leaned forward, resting her face against the polar bear's fur and looking up at the lights swirling and dancing through the sky. There were pictures in it now… Two bears, large and small. She laughed again quietly and stretched down one hand to stroke Peter's head.

Peter rubbed his muzzle against her hand lovingly and turned back to look at the pictures in the sky.

Sara reached out a hand towards the lights. Her mother's face… She was smiling…

"Sara?" A deep voice was calling her gently, and Sara blinked, not sure where she was. A moment ago, she'd been lying pillowed against the thick yellowish-white fur of a polar bear. She sat up a little, shaking her head, and stroked the fur under her fingers again – the furry lining of her grandad's hooded coat.

She was back! Back with Grandad – she was safe!

But it had been a dream then, she realized miserably. She hadn't saved Peter at all. She'd just woven it out of Grandad's story, and her own wish to be at home with her mother.

"I didn't mean to let you fall asleep, Sara, love," her grandad said gently. "I was telling the story, and remembering. It all seemed so real again, looking out at the snow. And when I glanced down, you'd drifted off. We'd better go back inside. Get you into a proper bed."

Sara nodded, standing up, and stretching out her fingers. Same old pink fleece gloves. Not caribou-fur mittens. She supposed they would have been hard to explain at school. She hefted her sleeping bag into her arms and the little packet of sandwiches, and smiled sadly up at Grandad.

"We never ate them."

"Never mind. I'll put them in the fridge. We might need them tomorrow, I think." Grandad took the bag, nodding mysteriously, but Sara wasn't listening.

"Grandad, look! My snow bear's gone. He's melted away."

There was only a shapeless snowy lump left behind. Sara's eyes filled with tears. Somehow that made it even worse – she didn't even have a snow bear cub any more. She sniffed and blinked the tears away, and the bright moonlight caught something sparkling in the snow outside the igloo.

Sara reached down and picked up the two pieces of green sea glass that had been her little bear's eyes. They glowed gently, with the soft green of the Northern Lights. She turned them over in her hand, her eyes widening. They'd changed. The green glow wasn't just the moonlight on the glass. It was *inside*, she was sure. And the glass was a different shape now – both pieces were paw prints, a little paw, and a great, heavy paw, soft triangles, edged with a ridge of claws.

Sara slipped them into her pocket. "Grandad? Can I keep the sea glass I used for his eyes?" she asked, smiling to herself.

"Course you can. I wonder why he melted so much faster than the rest of the snow?" Grandad said thoughtfully as they walked towards the house. "I don't think the roads will be clear till tomorrow morning."

Sara shook her head. Then she realized what Grandad had said and whirled round, dropping her sleeping bag in the snow. "The roads will be clear? Do you really think they will? You can take me home?"

Grandad picked it up, and put an arm round her. "I think I'd better. Your dad rang my mobile while you were asleep. You need to get home and meet your brother, and I want to spend Christmas with both my grandchildren." His eyes twinkled.

"Mum's had the baby already?" Sara gasped.

"Mm-hm. And they're calling him Peter." Grandad smiled at her as they hurried into the warmth of the cottage. "Just like my polar bear, Sara. I told you it was your dad's favourite story too." He put down the sleeping bag, and took hold of her hands. "You would have loved him, Sara, my little bear. I know it's silly, but I wish you could have met him."

Sara nodded, and wrapped her arms round Grandad's neck.

"I did…" she whispered, very, very quietly.

Also by Holly Webb:

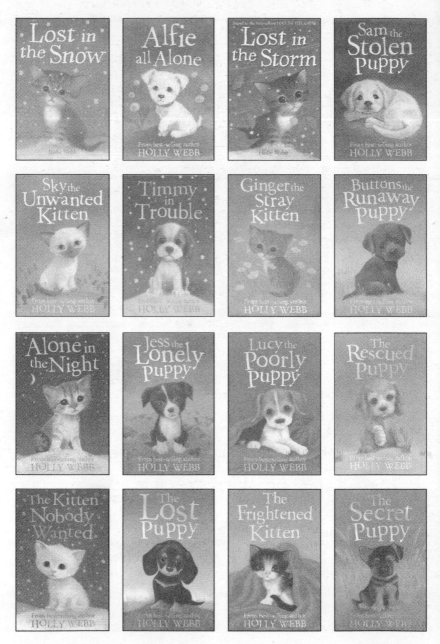

Lost in the Snow

Alfie all Alone
From best-selling author
HOLLY WEBB

Lost in the Storm

Sam the Stolen Puppy
From best-selling author
HOLLY WEBB

Sky the Unwanted Kitten
From best-selling author
HOLLY WEBB

Timmy in Trouble
HOLLY WEBB

Ginger the Stray Kitten
From best-selling author
HOLLY WEBB

Buttons the Runaway Puppy
HOLLY WEBB

Alone in the Night
From best-selling author
HOLLY WEBB

Jess the Lonely Puppy
From best-selling author
HOLLY WEBB

Lucy the Poorly Puppy
From best-selling author
HOLLY WEBB

The Rescued Puppy
From best-selling author
HOLLY WEBB

The Kitten Nobody Wanted
From best-selling author
HOLLY WEBB

The Lost Puppy
HOLLY WEBB

The Frightened Kitten
From best-selling author
HOLLY WEBB

The Secret Puppy
HOLLY WEBB